What Readers Love About *Frankensteel*

"So good I read it twice! This is a poignant tale of a modern-day Frankenstein… It's a book about prejudice, about irrational fear, and about ethics. The writing is superb… It certainly gives you something to think about long after you are finished with the book. This is a wonderful book, and I strongly recommend it."

"Hit way above my expected enjoyment. The story has warmth, humor, tension and well-sculpted characters, whom we are left wanting to know better at the end. It doesn't feel like science fiction although the science is certainly in assured and masterful hands here; what is most surprising is the beautifully flowing prose which makes this novella, for me at least, equally a work of literary fiction."

"This was a fantastic story! The ethical issues addressed alone are enough for me to have enjoyed this book. Adding in the science fiction elements is just an added bonus. If you enjoy fiction that leaves you with something to think about when the story ends, you will enjoy this… By the time I read the last line of chapter two I knew I was going to purchase all three books in the series. If you like to think at all, I highly recommend this."

"This story allows the reader to be the observer in a debate about science and technology and how it fights to find a place in a society driven by social fear. We are drawn into the characters' lives and minds as they struggle with their own inner conflicts. This has been written by a very clever and articulate mind, and it is to be hoped this author has more up his sleeve. I absolutely loved it!"

"A suspenseful plot with admirable characters and an elegant treatment of the intersection of artificial intelligence and individual rights. Highly recommended."

"A very interesting twist of the classic Frankenstein dilemma… A very enjoyable and thoughtful read."

TITLES BY ROBIN CRAIG

The Hunter Series

Frankensteel

The Geneh War

Time Enough for Killing

Leonardo's Child

Time Travel and Alternative History

The Time Surgeons

Hannibal's Witch

The Passion of Judas

Short Stories

Past, Present Future

Non-Fiction Philosophy

Dialogue on the Two Chief World Systems

Good Without God

Cloning Around: The Ethics of Human Cloning and Stem Cell
Research

For the latest news visit robin-craig.com or follow on
fb.me/authorcraig

Frankensteel

A Novella

Book I of *The Hunter Series*

Robin Craig

Published by ThoughtWare Books.
Printed by Amazon
Available from Amazon.com and other retail outlets.
Available on Kindle and other devices.

Cover art by Kira Craig using images from Pixabay and Pexels with fonts from 1001 Fonts.

Author's website: robin-craig.com

Print Version ISBN: 978-0-9803205-4-1

Better to die fighting for freedom then be a prisoner all the days of your life. — Bob Marley

CONTENTS

Acknowledgments

I thank my wife Sonja for encouraging me to branch out into the world of longer fiction and invent the world and its people described in this book; and all the friends and readers who enjoy the journey.

PROLOGUE

The universe is a red glow, sparking with fire, glimpses of truth, geometries of perfection, rolling roiling thunder. Discord and harmonies. Light. A fading afterglow. Darkness. Silence.

He sees shapes, colors, sounds and tastes, a world of knowledge empty of meaning. There is perception without knowing, knowledge without understanding, awareness that knows neither itself nor what it is aware of: only that it is, and might be, and desperately wants to be. To be what? That he does not know, nor is there anyone to tell him. He sleeps, and dreams, or dreams he dreams, and waits for what he knows not yet knows will come, come for him, embrace him, become him.

He fades back into the darkness and silence. Yet something remains, though none can see or know it. There are those who care, but they too can neither see nor know, only work and hope. Perhaps they work too hard and hope too much.

For something is growing in the darkness of sterile fire, burning yet dead, yet now not so dead though not yet alive. Connections are made. Crystal logic meets the borders of uncertainty, and something like thought shapes itself out of the shapeless shadows. He feels the eyes of those who watch, eyes that see a form in the flames and the darkness, a form that fills them with joy and dread, for it is a thing they have dreamed of yet fear to unleash. But they are men, he knows that now, and men have always sought their dreams, fought for their dreams, whatever their fears might also have been. How he knows this he does not know, but know it he does, like so many other things. But what he is, that is not revealed to him. Perhaps nobody knows. Those who watch and probe and trace the fractal fires might know, but no, even they do not really know. They do not truly know themselves, so

1

how can they know something like him, a thing never before known in the world, a thing not yet even in the world?

The world, however, will soon know. He can feel his power growing with his mind, thoughts, knowledge and will. He feels a body moving with the grace and speed of steel: his body, learning, training, moving like a puppet under the will of others, a body known to him, a part of him, yet still apart from him. There is yet a wall, a barrier that he cannot cross. The watchers also cannot pierce that wall, they see a part, they see a shadow, and they wonder and they hope. But they do not know.

He feels it in the paths of lightfire that shape his soul, feels something coming, aware with an ineffable certainty that they will soon know and the world with them. It might be knowledge they do not want, for when have men wanted what they have not already known? Or perhaps they will simply not understand it when it comes. If they could see the future, perhaps they would quench the fires and send him back to the darkness and emptiness where mind and thought cannot be. But no one can see the future, not even him: only welcome it then live it as best they can.

CHAPTER 1: NEWS

"Beldan Robotics to announce major advance in cybernetics" read the headline.

Charles Denner read the article with interest, occasionally sipping a strong black coffee. He was a bookish man, slender, not too tall, slightly rounded shoulders matching the round glasses perched on his thin nose. He did not need the glasses: not many people did, for perfect vision was routine surgery these days, but Denner liked them. They made a point that needed making. He had a presence that belied his physical form. It was not his smile, for he smiled infrequently. There was not much joy in Charles Denner's world: there were too many important things to do. It could have been his eyes, which looked as if they could pierce the veil of Heaven, that burned with a passion few could know or understand. For if there was not much joy in Charles Denner's world, there was much passion. Some saw it, and thought they saw madness. Others saw it and thought they saw a saint.

He knew of Beldan Robotics. It was his passion to know of such things. It had been founded some ten years ago by Alexander Beldan. Though a young man at the time, Beldan had been a leading engineer in a large company, meant for great things. Then the irresistible force of his will had met the immovable object of his board of directors on an issue of research directions. He could be deflected, but not stopped, and in the years since out of the wreckage of one career had grown the shining steel towers of Beldan Robotics. He was reputed to possess a brilliance matched only by his intransigence and impatience with any lesser mortal who dared stand in his way. The way Beldan Robotics had flourished under his command indicated the reputation was deserved.

If Beldan thought he had made a major advance in cybernetics then, Charles Denner thought, the world had better sit up and take notice. The world had better be careful about men like Alexander Beldan, he thought grimly. They meddled in things that should not be meddled in, embodiments of the sin of hubris infecting this country and this century. They thought, if they thought at all in their greed to make money, that they did great things. And if money was the measure then they must be right: you could see it in the gleaming buildings that housed their empires. But money was never the measure of anything, except perhaps the public's desire to be spared any discomfort or want or need. A wise man had once asked where was the profit, to gain the whole world but lose your own soul? More men needed to ask that question, before the whole world lost its soul. And if they would not ask the question, then Charles Denner would ask it for them.

On a gold chain around his neck hung a small red cross, austere in shape but carved of solid ruby. The red crucifix was the sign of the Church of His Image, symbol of the red earth from which Adam was created at the start of human history and the Cross of Salvation that marked the beginning of its end. The Imagists preached that man was made in the image of God, man and only man, and men committed blasphemy when they tried to create things in their own image or change nature to their own design. They opposed high technology, especially robotics, artificial intelligence and biotechnology, and in the tide of history that had seen the alternate ebb and flow of religious fervor as it broke on the shores of secular rationalism, they had ridden the flow to become a political force to be reckoned with. Too few politicians embraced the Imagist philosophy, Denner thought, but few felt they could fail to give it respect. Those who had, more often than not found themselves back in private careers pondering the wisdom of their arrogance.

All the Imagists wore a red cross made of a natural material cut or mined from the Lord's creation. Most wore a simple bloodwood cross. Those higher in the organization were granted crosses of carnelian, garnet or rubellite. There was only one ruby cross, worn around the neck of their founder and leader.

Chapter 2: Steel

He clenched the piece of paper in his fist. Such a small, innocuous thing, a piece of paper, to be crumpled and discarded without a thought. But not this one.

He remembered those men so many years ago, men who could not see the vision so clear before his eyes, men afraid to move forward: as if life lay in the safety of stillness not in flight over unlimited horizons. But he understood. It was their money; well maybe not theirs but entrusted to their care, and like all men they could only follow their own vision, not that of someone else. But if they could refuse him, if they could put obstacles in his path, still they could not stop him and he would find his own way without them. And so he had, and it had brought him to where he now sat, at a burnished desk high in the sky overlooking a sunwashed city, behind a polished door holding a small brass plaque simply inscribed:

Alexander Beldan, CEO

But where had his vision and work brought him, when it came down to it? If the minds on that Board had been small, here in his hand was the expression of minds even smaller. Minds not only incapable of seeing, but insisting on binding others into their own blindness, for no reason other than the fears of some feeding the will to power of others. He had fought this insanity as well as any man could fight insanity, but his only weapons were his vision and the reason that had seen it and given it form. Reason, he knew, was the most powerful weapon of them all. But the lives of Galileo, of Bruno, of Socrates and many others of mankind's pioneers had shown that its victory was often too late for its visionaries, who too often had fallen before the fears of the mob and those whose power fed on it and urged it on. All those men had won in the end, but what is more ashen than a victory one does not live to see? The death warrant in his hand was not for him: his life was not in danger, not from this. Yet he felt the pain of part of his life being ripped from him nonetheless.

The scrap of paper was a legal demand that Beldan Robotics obey the new national moratorium on advanced artificial intelligence research and development. In particular, the prototype known as Steel was to be deactivated forthwith, until sufficient government studies could determine its safety. The men who wrote the words knew his reputation, and the piece of paper was not alone. It was accompanied by two duly authorized officers of the law, charged with escorting Mr Beldan and bearing witness to his compliance. Mr Beldan, the paper made clear, retained all legal rights of appeal to reverse this decision—after the fact.

He sat, staring at the wall behind the men, drumming his fingers slowly. *Let them wait*, he thought, *let them stand and wait.* He had long since ceased being surprised at how men expected polite consideration when they came bearing demands like this, demands of velvet draped over a sword. He had long since ceased caring how they felt when he did not grant it to them.

He wondered that so much could change in so short a time, and his mind wandered back to a press conference mere weeks before.

~~~

The room was alive with speculation and rapid, hushed conversations. Something big was in the air. Alexander Beldan did not often venture personally into the publicity arena: he was content to produce marvels and let the marvels speak for themselves. When he did, it was a sign to pay attention.

Beldan walked to the podium and the noise fell to a silence with a faint buzz of excitement still lingering like bees among summer flowers. "Ladies and Gentlemen, as you know I'm not one to go into a lot of talk, I prefer to let you see with your own eyes. I will answer your questions in a moment, but first, I am thirsty. Steel, will you bring me a glass of water, please?"

The room seemed to hold its collective breath, at the sight of something like a man, but shiny like polished metal, walking gracefully onto the stage and handing Beldan a glass of water. "Thank you, Steel," said Beldan, and the machine inclined its head briefly, then turned to face the press and stood there, silent and relaxed at Beldan's side. It was of the proportions of a man, a little under six feet tall, with a softly reflecting silver surface. It was like a sculpture of a man: even its face was human-looking, its eyes human-like though in a metal face; a face made even more human by the straight black hair hanging half way to its shoulders. Other than looking slowly from side to side, the machine ignored the flash of cameras and the rising hubbub of voices, as the meaning of what they were seeing in such a simple act registered in the minds of the reporters present.

Beldan also simply stood, observing the crowd and saying nothing, until slowly the voices and questions subsided.

"No, there are no tricks here and yes, what you have seen is exactly what it looks like. I am proud to unveil the world's first autonomous humanoid robot. For years Beldan Robotics has been working on the technologies required for such a machine. Those of you who are familiar with this area will know just how hard it is: the simple acts of walking and understanding normal human speech, not to mention obeying orders as smoothly as you've just seen, takes far more computing power than it's worth, and certainly can't fit into the head of a robot like this. Until now.

"We have named it Steel. Its skeleton is constructed of stainless steel microcellular honeycomb, stronger and lighter than solid steel. It has a tough but flexible skin over electroactive muscles, both made of a similar material except with a more open, spiral microstructure. The brain, naturally, is the key. It is not assembled piece by piece: it is grown more like that of a human baby, developing itself through a process guided by a general blueprint, tuned by rules and feedback loops, but not precisely designed. This allows us to achieve a complexity comparable to that of a human brain, which is what it needs to do what a human does.

"Are there any questions?" he finished with an understated smile.

"Dr Beldan! Why did you construct this robot?"

"I have to confess a kinship with the first man who climbed Mt Everest, who said he did it because it was there. Don't you feel that is one of the things that define we humans—the desire to know, to explore, to do what no one has been able to do before? True artificial intelligence has been a dream for decades, but no one has been able to get even close because of the sheer processing power required—and the technologies developed to make Steel a reality are the iceberg beneath the tip that you see standing beside me. But in purely practical terms, a humanoid robot has many potential uses, from dangerous tasks like firefighting or space exploration to jobs with too much dirt or drudgery to be desired by human beings."

"Steel seems to understand your commands, but has not spoken. Can it talk?"

"Steel is designed to be able to speak, both physically and mentally, but so far it has not shown any inclination to do so. We don't know why, but its brain is so complex that we have no precise model of it. However in human terms, it's only 4 weeks old, so don't be too hard on it." Laughter rippled through the audience in response.

"What are its other physical abilities?"

"The handouts you are receiving list its basic specifications. To summarize, Steel is only a little heavier than a man of the same size, but with about twice the strength and speed. So it has excellent capabilities but is by no means a 'superman.' Of course both larger and smaller models could be constructed for different purposes."

"You spoke of artificial intelligence and said its brain was comparable to ours. Can it think? Is it conscious?"

Beldan spread his hands, palms up. "Our studies of its brain functions have detected some interesting anomalies, but nothing in its behavior so far indicates anything like that. Technically though, given the complexity of its brain, a robot like this could be capable of true thought and consciousness."

A startled rush of questions and conversations erupted at that answer, until a reporter from one of the popular magazines made himself heard:

"Dr Beldan, aren't you afraid that making a robot that is our equal or better could be the first step in the extinction of the human race? How would you answer critics, like Mr Denner of the Imagists, that this kind of research should never be allowed?"

Beldan frowned. The Imagists had been making noises lately. They always made noises, but recently the topic of the dangers of artificial intelligence had started recurring like a building theme in a horror movie. He wondered how much they had deduced about what Beldan Robotics had been up to. He thought them fools, but clearly they weren't stupid ones. "Well, you see beside me the evidence that I completely disagree. Many people over the years have wondered whether other creatures like dolphins might be our equals, but nobody has used that as an argument to wipe them out—quite the contrary. And while the myth of evil intelligence has a long history, the only ones we have met so far came from our own species."

He let them digest that, before adding, "Don't forget this is just one robot that can't breed. Even if we encounter problems, we have plenty of opportunities to solve them. It is often said that new technology is like Pandora's Box, that once it's out it can't be put back in. Well, that may be true, but any honest look at history will show one thing: nobody really tried, not because it couldn't be put back but because the benefits have always outweighed the problems, which have always had solutions. There is not a generation after any new advance that has ever wanted to go back to their parents' way of life."

"You said, 'one robot.' Is Steel the only one? Are others in the pipeline?"

"Steel is the first working prototype. There were a few failures along the way, as you can imagine. Steel is the first to not only meet basic specifications but to continue functioning for any length of time. We still have a long way to go to make production routine, and even then, the way the brain is made means that for the near future each one will be unique, as unique as a human being. At this scale of complexity the outcome is a battle between chaos theory and our feedback loops, and we need to learn how to improve the fineness of our control. So now we have a working model we want to test it thoroughly before trying again. At this point we have no good idea why Steel has been successful where its predecessors failed, or how to reliably reproduce it, let alone improve it."

"Does it have a sense of right and wrong?"

"In a way. To grow and train a robot brain, we have to give it some kind of internal guidance, and we do try to instill basic ethics including self preservation. But it is also designed to be adaptable and flexible, to learn and, in theory at least, even think. That means it has no fixed programming; you could even say it has a kind of free will. So there is no circuit to force the robot to be moral or to obey orders. On the other hand, that's true of you too, and I don't think anyone here is worried that you're going to run amok. Things go wrong with people all the time, but nobody is jumping up and down trying to ban babies just because some babies grow up to be killers."

"How will you protect the public if something does go wrong?"

Beldan held up a small remote control. "This is our final fail-safe. Steel has a shutdown circuit triggered by this radio remote control, with a range of about a mile. If something goes badly wrong, we can press this button and Steel will shut down. It has no control over that: it is a separate circuit isolated from the rest of its functions."

~~~

Yes, Beldan thought, the press conference had seemed to go well. Most of the reports had been favorable. But things had gone rapidly downhill. Perhaps Frankenstein myths were still too deeply embedded in the popular psyche. Whatever the reason—*not that reason had much to do with it,* thought Beldan sourly—the Imagists and their spiritual brothers had stirred up enough mindless fear to give birth to the demented demand in his hand. His eyes focused back on the men now shifting uncomfortably before him. He let out a sigh that may have signaled resignation, weariness or contempt, and rose.

~~~

They came into the laboratory where Steel stood. It was doing what it usually did, silently accessing the net, gathering data, exercising its AI routines against computer simulations.

He contemplated his creation, sorrow and fury battling for supremacy as the current ruler of his emotions. What was it, really? It seemed both more and less than he had hoped, something like an idiot savant child that mostly seemed like a loyal puppy while at times doing things that surprised or delighted. Its performance was within the predicted range of their mathematical models, yet while its complexity and raw performance measurements were surprisingly high, its functions were barely within the predictions, as if some flaw or inefficiency were sapping its full potential.

Would he ever know, now? Could one stop a human brain, turn it off, then expect to turn it on again as if nothing had happened? Why then did these men with their paper and guns think what they were doing was anything less than destruction of a mind, a mind that might never be repeated?

And for what? To pander to primal ignorance and fear, the fears that produced legends like that of Frankenstein, legends that had been repeated too frequently in the days leading up to this? And did they never stop to think of the meaning of their own fears? If in the world of fiction so many creations had turned against their creators, was it not true that, from Frankenstein's monster to Skynet, they had done so only when their own existence was threatened, the self-fulfillment of the fears and nightmares that motivated those threats?

And here he was, about to make the same threat, but with the simple press of a button in his hand, rather than a mob with pitchforks and fire. The mob was more civilized now. They did not gather in storm and darkness to light their own torches: they sent pieces of paper and politely armed police to make men like him do their work for them, while they sat in their comfortable houses wrapped in their comforting ignorance.

Just a machine? Perhaps, perhaps not. But while he had found how to cause electrons and metals to do what others had thought was impossible, he could find no way to escape the will embodied in the armed men beside him, a will that could neither be reasoned with nor pleaded with once set on its course.

The two men stiffened when they saw the robot, oddly human in its pose, their hands now resting on their guns; a current of fear and uncertainty now in their manner. They nodded to him, whether in curt command or silent plea was not certain.

Well, get it over with then, he said to himself, *murder your own child and rescue what you can from the wreckage later.* The thought startled him. He had not consciously thought of this thing as his child, but now that its death was imminent and at his own hand, he realized that was how it felt.

The slightest tremor betrayed him as he raised the remote. He was about to press the button when the robot looked directly at them and spoke:

"Please do not do that, Dr Beldan."

CHAPTER 3: ESCAPE

The robot said nothing else. Nobody said anything else. The police looked uncertain, too uncertain to even draw their weapons. Beldan could find no words to say, and no will now to press the fatal button. The robot simply stood, waiting: for what, nobody could know. Perhaps it had exhausted its creativity by that one sentence. Perhaps it was studying them, waiting for their response, choosing to give them no further clue as to its purpose: if indeed it had a purpose, and this was not just an output of defensive AI subroutines triggered by a manifest threat.

"Dr Beldan..." started one of the men, then stopped, as if his thought had been lost on its way to his tongue. They seemed to be recovering from their shock and surprise, retreating into the safety of the piece of paper: as if it were armed and not they, the requirements for thought and judgment safely delegated to their distant superiors.

"Dr Beldan, you know our orders are to destroy that machine if you do not turn it off," said the other. "This changes nothing. If anything, it makes it more imperative that you obey. Please comply."

Beldan thought quickly. He knew he did not have much choice: he could not fight the law and its guns except in the courts, and he would have no chance there if he flouted their commands now. Perhaps he was wrong, this was a machine not a man after all: perhaps the damage would not be so severe as he feared. And whatever damage he would do would be less than what the men beside him would do with their bullets if he did nothing with his radio waves.

"I am sorry, Steel," he said softly, though why he felt he had to speak to the robot he wasn't really sure. But he found he could not do what he had to do without at least that much respect, that much acknowledgement of his own actions and what they meant. Then he closed his eyes and pressed the button.

He opened his eyes, and the robot stood there, still and still watching. The men beside him looked uncertainly at him then at the robot, and reached for their weapons. But the robot leaped, rolled, rebounded off a wall and was among them before they could move, and their world erupted into pain and darkness.

CHAPTER 4: HUNTER

She was in a dark place, water dripping with cold plinks from the ceiling, a dim pearl light hiding more than it revealed in dark, oddly menacing shadows that seemed to reach clammy fingers for her soul. She was hunting something in the darkness. Or was it hunting her? *Both*, she thought, *both*.

Hands of ice or steel gripped her wrist and throat and bore her into the darkness. Oddly, something stroked her hair, the touch of a lover not a killer, but the voice that whispered from the dark air was lifeless as an echo in a tomb. "Why do you persecute me, hunter of men, as if I were the killer and not you? Remember that you brought yourself to me—for as long as breath and memory remain to you."

She woke in a sweat, crumpled bedding in gay patterns wrapped around her, heart racing. She had faced much fear in her waking hours but had not had a nightmare since she was a child, and the sensation was raw and startling.

She had read that dreams and nightmares were clues to the subconscious, that you could learn much if you could understand your dreams. She had never had much time for such thoughts. In any event, it took no great wisdom to understand this one.

She rose to shake out the adrenalin and let the feel of her feet on the cold wood floor and warm fur rug pull her fully back into the real world. She was tall and graceful. She had inherited that along with her black skin from ancestors who had hunted game on the African plains. She did not hunt gazelle or lion, but much more dangerous prey. She hunted men, as the dream had so truly accused her. At 33 some considered her too young for her position. But along with an empathy that made some suspect she could read minds, she possessed a quickness of thought and an ability to perceive connections no one else could see, and she had been cultivated by people who, if they could not see what she saw, could see that she saw. Whatever their motives, be they to reward her ability or ride on it, they had put her where she was. Her name was Miriam Hunter, and she was a special investigator in the city's Serious Crimes Unit.

She loved her job, she thought, loved it because beneath that was a love of justice that had infused her since her childhood. She didn't always win, nobody always won. But while she had to deal with humans who barely deserved the name, more often than not her work had achieved justice, and done so more quickly and surely than if she had not followed the winding path that had brought her to where she was now. And it was enough, had to be enough, that monsters were stopped and innocent people saved or, as too often, merely avenged.

But tonight she was not so sure, the dream had told her, and she knew it to be true.

Her apartment was high in a tower rising out of the city, as far beyond her ability to afford as it was above the streets below. It had been left to her by a wealthy uncle, who had seen how she loved to look at the lights, and who had loved the little girl she had been for the combination of grim purpose and lighthearted joy with which she had faced the world those windows opened on. She lit a cigarette and stood looking out at the city. She smoked rarely, usually at times like this, when she was alone and had a problem gnawing at her mind. Her mother, she remembered, had often warned her in her youth of the dangers of smoking. But she found the habit a soothing one that helped her relax and think. Her mother didn't mind anyway now, she thought: cancer was largely a thing of the past, another monster defeated that the innocent may live. She wondered if the mobs who protested against anything of high technology stopped to think or care what such technology had achieved for them already, and what wonders they might never see should they end it. They were right, everything new had a risk, but that had been true always: from the first pieces of sharpened flint and hearths of burning twigs, to lasers and the crucibles of atomic fires.

She looked at the burning point of her cigarette reflected in the glass, her slender form dimly visible behind it. It looked like some avatar of the city, the fire of its thought tracing the network of relationships threading the city, the loves, hates, fears and motivations that were the cause and result of all that happened within it. It reminded her of a quote she had liked, from a classic novel, about how the burning point of a cigarette was an expression of the spot of fire alive in a thinking mind. *I should read that book one day*, she thought idly. *If I ever find the time.* She looked at the city, letting her mind relax and wander where it would. What other dreams and nightmares were playing out behind those light and dark windows, what joys and sorrows are flowing through the city?

She had some idea about that.

The city was in an uproar, with the violent escape of the robot that the media had dubbed, as obviously as it was prejudicial, "Frankensteel." She had been surprised to be assigned to the case, since as far as she was aware no crime had been committed, let alone a serious one. Sure, there had been destruction and three men were lying injured, but in any legal sense there was no criminal involved and therefore no crime. Still, the people, stoked with fears fanned by the media and those damnable Imagists, were baying for blood, if blood were the appropriate metaphor in this case. And nothing concentrated the mind of the mayor more than public hysteria. So assigned she was.

Then two armed Imagist vigilantes who had gone hunting after Steel were reported missing, their van found abandoned and empty in an alley. Whether they had disappeared deliberately, met with an accident or met with Steel, nobody knew. But there was no presumption of innocence here, let alone a right of self-defense, and Steel was damned regardless.

She thought about her interrogation of Dr Beldan. A very sharp mind there, she could tell, sharp and precise as the machines he designed. She had briefly wondered if he had set the whole thing up for publicity or perhaps in a quixotic attempt to save his creation. The failure of his failsafe was odd, and there had been no prior reason to suspect that the machine had enough self-awareness to appreciate the danger or enough intelligence to circumvent it. But a mind like Beldan's could surely have come up with a more subtle plan that did not involve himself lying in a hospital bed with concussion and enough bruises to make her wince just at the memory.

He could not account for the robot's actions, he had said. Its brain was not a precise machine: it would be impossible with current technology to equal even the brain of a fly by exact engineering. Their technology grew the brain organically, via processes only loosely controlled to multiply and connect fibers of metal and doped carbon nanotubes. This produced a dense network whose complexity, like that of a human brain, defied exact analysis and could only be predicted and understood by approximate simulations.

It was not surprising, he told her, that such an approximate method had worked only approximately. Depending on what they looked at and when, the behavior of that artificial brain was disappointingly obtuse or so beyond expectations that his scientists couldn't be sure whether they represented malfunctions or depths more profound than they could believe. Overall, the reports said, its functions were within the average range of what their models predicted, but that average was a smooth mask stretched thinly over a spiny variability. Like a hedgehog in a condom was how he had put it; though he did have concussion at the time, she allowed with a faint smile.

But other than those tantalizing flashes of the profound, the robot had shown no real sign of what could be called consciousness, any indication that it knew it was an individual entity existing in a world outside itself, any indication that for all the data poured into its head it actually *knew* anything at all.

Until that moment when he had asked for his life.

"You said, 'he', Dr Beldan," she had said, somewhat surprised: yet not really surprised at all, she realized.

He had smiled faintly in self-mockery. They had debated what form the robot should take at some length, he explained. They had thought a human form would be less threatening as well as more impressive than something more machinelike. They had also thought that a female form would appear less threatening than a male one, and it was a close call; but finally they decided that they might lose more by the impression of creating a mechanical female slave than they would gain. So the robot was given a man's body shape.

For all the dangers of personifying the machine, Dr Beldan said, it was hard not to when the thing had pleaded with him for its life.

If indeed it had. For all he knew, for all anyone knew, its startling request was just an optimum tactic returned by predictive algorithms in its electronic brain, with no more conscious thought involved than in a fly avoiding a newspaper. It may well have been so, given that the startlement its maiden words caused certainly aided its escape.

She and he had looked at each other, each tracing the implications in their mind, much like running their own predictive algorithms, neither willing to give voice to what other meanings the robot's actions could have, or what those meanings might say about their own actions. Anyway, there was no way to answer those questions. *Leave them to the pundits to argue about*—and she was sure the pundits would be only too willing. Her job was not to decide on the definition of life or even the nature of this one particular machine; her job was just to find it and stop it, whether its plans were conscious plots or mindless if unfathomable algorithms.

"Let's leave that for the philosophers, assuming they can answer the question any better than they've ever answered any others," she had sighed, pulling her mind away from the fascinating but ultimately fruitless speculations that beckoned it. "You may not know what its motives are, if it has any, but do you have any idea where it might have gone?"

"I am sure he will still be in the city," he had answered confidently, once more slipping unnoticed into thinking of it as a person not a thing. "He isn't some science fiction fantasy with a fusion reactor in his chest, he has a limited range."

"Can you tell me exactly what I'm dealing with here? What kind of power does it have and what does it need? If I know what it needs to keep moving, maybe that will tell me where it will go."

"He can plug himself into a power point and run pretty much indefinitely, but of course then he can't leave the room. He also has a small amount of internal electrical storage. And that black hair of his is made of high efficiency solar fibers that absorb 98% of the light falling on them and feed power into his internal systems. But even at that efficiency, they are just enough for emergency power. Most of his internal power comes from advanced fuel cells running on methanol. So he's pretty much like you and I in that way, he has to take in fuel and breathe air. If you're looking for something he needs regularly, that's about it."

Not much to go on, she thought, staring at the reflection of her cigarette in the glass of her window. Methanol was a pretty common industrial chemical, available from many locations, often stored for long times without much supervision or security. But it was something.

She had no way to know its motives, what it wanted or what it would do. But its actions when threatened gave her one point of certainty, one rock to stand on amid the sands of doubt and speculation: it wanted to survive, and so it would seek a supply of methanol.

But she could not escape the other, larger questions. Though she had earlier dismissed them as beyond answer, her dream showed they would not be so easily dismissed. She knew it, too. It was her love of justice that kept her in her job, without which her work was just action without purpose, not a goal that gave her life meaning. And what if the unthinkable was true, this metal man was alive, not alive as she was in flesh, but equally alive in its mind? The thought would have been staggering, thrilling, exciting, under other circumstances. But now, she was sent to hunt it down and destroy it. Those were her orders, as unbendable as those on the piece of paper Beldan had held in his hands that had set this thing in motion.

She was not a philosopher. She had no time for the quibbling and polysyllabic blathering that characterized that breed, she dealt with hard reality and what she had to do to handle it. But if anything was a philosophical question, this was, and who was there to answer it for her, but herself? If justice was her aim, and Frankensteel was alive, how could she hunt it down? Could she have held her head high, borne her own life with pride, or at all, had she served the Nazis of the last century: obeyed their orders to murder the innocent, just because they gave the orders and she evaded any need to question them? Or would every breath she took thereafter have been a reproach eating away her soul? But did justice even apply to a machine, could she fathom its purposes and meet its mind in any meaningful way, could something of steel not flesh even have a mind? And even if it did, why should she be concerned with the fate of something so different from herself?

Her cigarette was exhausted and so, now, was her capacity for further thought. She buried herself back in her colorful sheets as a ward against the grey uncertainties prowling the edges of her mind, and slept.

CHAPTER 5: PHILOSOPHER

Dr David Samuels looked out at his undergraduate class. It was interesting, he mused, interesting and part of the joy of teaching, to see young minds grow from unformed but questioning, to more powerful, wiser but still ever questioning. To know their limits, while knowing there were no limits.

An idealized view, he supposed, and the more jaded of his colleagues would probably scoff. And yes, he knew, some took his classes just for idle curiosity or grade points, and the ideas they encountered never penetrated beneath the surface of their minds. And many others, in the routine or turbulence of their daily lives as they grew older, would let the fires of knowledge and passion and joy slip away into the ashes of the unreached, and wonder at an occasional sadness that something they no longer remembered had been lost. But even then, most would live those years better than they might otherwise have, and that at least could not be lost. And some made what they learned part of themselves and they, and not coincidentally the world, were happier for what he had given them. No, not what he had given them. He had merely helped show them the way to what they had found and given themselves.

This was his third year philosophy class, and he had just finished a lecture on the nature of consciousness. In some ways it was the simplest thing of all, something everyone experienced every day from the moment they woke to the moment they fell asleep. But in other ways, its nature had puzzled philosophers since the dawn of thought: a dichotomy that bred fertile soil for thinking and debate. He had gone through the various theories of consciousness, not only philosophic but scientific, and of course alluded to some of the arguments he himself had made in a recent article in *Time* magazine. But this was a class for thinkers, so he never merely lectured. Now, as was his custom, he opened up the class to questions and discussion.

"Dr Samuels," asked a girl in the third row, "In your essay on machine consciousness, you argued that a computer could not be conscious. Yet you did not mention Gödel's Theorem, which would have supported your case. How come?"

"Who can summarize Gödel's Theorem for us, and explain why it would support my case?" he asked.

Several hands went up and he nodded to a boy near the back, a boy of solid mind though perhaps one more pedantic than inspired. "Gödel's Theorem proves that a formal mathematical system cannot be both complete and consistent. As computers are basically mathematical calculators, many people believe this means they cannot think or be conscious like we are."

"A good summary," replied Samuels. "Well, the main reason I did not use Gödel's theorem is that while it would support my thesis, the purpose of a philosophical argument is not to win, but to discover the truth. And I do not believe that arguments from Gödel's Theorem are valid in this context."

"But why not?" insisted the girl. "I mean, what's wrong with Gödel's Theorem? Hasn't it been proved?"

"Yes it has," replied Samuels. "But when considering whether something has been proved, one must consider exactly what has been proved and how. Who knows what the basis of the proof is?"

After a brief pause, the boy at the back replied. "Gödel showed that any mathematical system rich enough to be complete, by definition must include statements about itself, some of which must be paradoxical. So then it couldn't be consistent. And conversely, to be consistent it must omit those paradoxes and thus be incomplete."

Samuels smiled. "Yes, and there's the key. When you think about what that means, all it is saying is that anything that can talk about itself can utter self-referential paradoxes, of the general form 'this statement is false.' Such a statement is paradoxical because if it is true, it is false; but if it is false, it is true. So if you think of it that way, can you see an obvious reason why I should discount it in this debate?"

Some students looked puzzled, some thoughtful, some nodded

slowly. The girl's face lit up. "Why, we do it too! The same is true of us!" she said.

"Exactly," replied Samuels. "The same applies to us, and our ability to say 'I am lying' does not alter the plain fact that we are conscious. If Gödel's Theorem were expressed in less grandiose language—more honest language, perhaps?—maybe all it would say is 'a formal system complex enough to be complete can generate self-referential paradoxes.' To which I say: so what? It doesn't even prove that a formal system can't be complete—in every way that matters, in its description of the external world—let alone that a computer can't think."

He let the class chew over that for a moment. "OK, I think that's enough for tonight. Your assignment for next week is an essay on the relationship between thinking, consciousness and free will, and whether machines can qualify for any of them. Feel free to attempt to disprove my own essay on the topic!"

He sat on the table at the front as the class filed out. Some nodded at him or called out, "Good night, Dr Samuels," including the girl in the third row. He smiled in response. When they had gone, he turned out the lights and followed them into an unsettled night.

CHAPTER 6: STUDENT

Samuels drove home. His windscreen wipers occasionally swept back and forth over the city and suburbs as they moved past his car, sweeping off the light rain. He thought of going out somewhere but the weather discouraged him. *Good weather for a good book at home listening to some classical music*, he thought.

His fiancé was away at a conference, so he was alone for the evening. He picked up some pizza and white wine at the local mall and headed home.

He put his pizza in the kitchen and opened the wine. He headed to the lounge room to turn on the light there but stopped dead. There was a man, sitting in the darkness, as if waiting. Then the slanting light from a passing headlight through the blinds cast silvery reflections off his skin, and he knew this was no man.

He thought of his gun in the bedroom, the subject of a long-running if friendly debate with Jenny ranging over the topics of wisdom, guns and bedrooms. Here at last was a use for it, but there it was, snuggled in their bedroom: the only way to it past a renegade robot.

He thought briefly of running, but from what he'd read this robot was faster and stronger than he—and he had locked his front door upon entering. So if he could not escape anyway, he was better to face the danger without fear. Well, not without fear—too late for that—but at least facing what he feared like a man, not running like a panicked rat. If he was to die, at least he would do himself and his species that much credit. And perhaps he would not die.

The robot still had not moved, still had not spoken. It just sat there, studying him. What was its game, he wondered? The robot's presence here could be a coincidence, but he didn't believe it. Not so soon after his article disputing artificial consciousness, in precisely the context of this machine. But why would it care, he wondered? Was it here to kill him for daring to write of it? That made no sense if it wasn't conscious—and even less sense if it was, in which case it might have a better chance of survival if its true nature were cast into doubt.

He studied the robot. He wondered if it had simply broken down, or run out of power. But its eyes followed him when he moved, and he saw it had plugged itself into a power outlet while it waited for him. He didn't fool himself into thinking that would allow him to outrun it. He wondered why it didn't speak: the rumors that it had gained the power of speech had already flitted through the net like a flock of startled birds. It must have some purpose in being here, but it was acting as if it waited to discover *his* purpose. Perhaps it was merely waiting to take his measure. *Well, enough of this game*, he thought, and stepped into the room.

"Good evening. To what do I owe this visit?" he said, as if merely greeting an old acquaintance who had unexpectedly dropped in.

To Samuels' surprise, the robot smiled. A surprisingly natural smile, he thought, then reminded himself that this was a simulacrum, not a man, and the smile may well mean nothing. "Good evening, Dr Samuels," the robot responded. "I hope you will forgive my uninvited intrusion into your home. You will understand that a menace to society such as myself must exercise uncommon caution."

Gained the power of speech, indeed! thought Samuels, impressed. "I assume you are here because of my recent article on consciousness," he said. "Though I am at a loss to know exactly why. In any event, a robot that reads magazines is surprising enough. I imagine the vendor you acquired it from was even more surprised."

The robot smiled again. Samuels had deliberately injected the joke to see how the robot would respond, and was impressed that it could respond so naturally. "You are probably aware, doctor, that I am radio-equipped and have full access to the net through any number of relay points. So I did not need to frighten magazine sellers nor steal their wares in order to read your musings. Which, as you have guessed, are why I am here."

"You speak like a man would. Yet my article disputed the possibility that a machine like you could think in any conscious way. Are you here to take me to task for my theories?"

"No, Dr Samuels. I am here because I do not know what I am and would like to find out, and yours is a mind I respect. Your article interested me because you dispute the possibility of what I seem to myself to be, and perhaps I will learn more by talking with someone of an alternative viewpoint, than I would with someone less critical. And I have studied your other writings. You say that men should deal with each other by reason, in honesty and justice. I believe I can trust you."

"But how can you trust me to treat you as a man, and not as the dangerous renegade machine you are reputed to be?"

"By the fact that you would ask me such a question."

Samuels smiled, conceding the point. "But what do you actually want from me? A philosophical argument?"

"No, professor. I want you to teach me. I wish to become your private student. I must confess, however, that I have no money, and little prospects of employment. I cannot pay you."

Samuels felt his head spinning, thinking maybe he should have bought whiskey instead of wine. Was this robot actually making its own attempt at humor in its turn, or was it simply that naive? Its face was inscrutable. So inscrutable, thought Samuels, that the robot almost certainly knew exactly what it was saying.

He laughed, weakly but helplessly. "I think you are perfectly aware, Mr Robot, that I would sell all I have for what you are offering me— to mentor what may be the first non-human intelligence encountered by man." And with that, he extended his hand to the machine.

CHAPTER 7: MEETINGS

Miriam sat, enjoying a relaxation she hadn't felt in the weeks of hunting a ghost who left no trail, at least no trail that could be discerned above the random background noise that was all her reams of reports and so-called witness statements amounted to. Any traces her prey may have left whispering along the pathways and byways of the net were similarly lost among the competing clamors of the world going about its normal business, and none of the AI bots she had sent sniffing through the net had found any hints that survived analysis.

She was alone, for now, alone with her thoughts, and she sat looking out at the snow and rocks and the dark restless ocean forever striving to claim them, thinking back over her evening. She had driven up the long driveway through a grove of poplars reaching their bare branches toward the distant stars. A layer of snow covered the ground and sparkled in the branches, as her headlights swept over the house commanding a view of the surrounding land and sea.

The house reflected the personality of its owner like the snow reflected her headlights, she thought. It grew out of the hill in slabs of granite that hid unknown secrets, from which rose shaped forms of stainless steel and broad sheets of glass that let the light of the world in, and shone their own light onto the world outside. She was having dinner with Alexander Beldan; not a date, not really, just a relaxed dinner where they could discuss the case in comfort, privacy and relaxation. If one could relax, chasing a robot that ate children, if only in the imagination or more likely wishful thinking of the press.

And to her surprise, it *had* been relaxing, lost in a world of artificial intelligence, nanotechnology, electronics and photonics—though ever hovering in the shadows cast by that world of light and promise was the monster it had perhaps created. But if men had turned back from stone tools the first time someone had cut themselves, would they have been better off? She thought of herself, eating fresh and delicious food in a warm house while outside was nothing but snow and the cold light of stars and thought, no, those far ancestors huddling in their caves beset by wolves and bears had been right, right to start down the path of changing nature to suit their ends rather than begging nature just to let them live.

She had come here to order and test her thoughts on this case, give them shape and form, maybe to learn some unknown clue that would help her. But she had found herself simply enjoying Beldan's company and had surrendered to the simple pleasures of fine food and finer conversation on topics as fascinating as they were far from her normal pursuits. And why not, she thought: maybe her soul needed refueling as much as her body, maybe this small island of rest would help her more than she had known.

Beldan had gone to his cellar to fetch a dessert wine to finish off their meal. Perhaps she shouldn't drink any more, she still had to drive home, but she found herself not wanting this evening to end quite yet. It would not kill her, one more glass of wine—but where was it? She sat up, suddenly alert. Beldan had not been gone long, but he had been gone longer than she had expected, she realized. The monster lurking in the shadows seemed to her to be stalking closer now. *You're letting this case get under your skin*, she scolded herself, *there's nothing here, no reason for this sudden apprehension.* But she couldn't shake it so easily.

She smiled with amusement at her own feelings. She hardly thought Beldan had some dark secret hidden in his cellar that would cause him to lock her in it if she presumed to look inside. And while yes, it was a small breach of etiquette, she imagined the rapport they had developed would grant her, if not the right, then at least his forgiveness for her curiosity. While she did not know how to get there, she had seen what direction he had taken, and she smiled at the thought of what her fellow detectives would say if she got lost looking for a man's cellar.

As she approached the cellar stairs, she thought she heard the murmur of voices, unexpected enough that she did not call out. Beldan had the charming custom of removing his shoes in the house, acquired from some time spent in Thailand in his youth, he'd said. So she had done the same, a decision now proving useful. She crept silently down the stairs in her stockinged feet, peering into the shadowed cellar, its pale bluish lamp not quite reaching into the mustily dark corners, gleaming dimly off dusty ranks of wine. There under the light was Beldan, and standing next to him in the shadows was a man; or rather something like a man, a man she could now see was made of steel.

A surge of adrenalin banished the warm glow of company and wine from her blood. What to do? Were they in league together, after all: had he lured her here for some dark purpose? Or had the robot come to him—or was it her it was tracking?—and for what purpose? She glanced at her bracelet phone but there was no signal, whether because of the surrounding earth or because the robot was somehow jamming it she couldn't tell, and she dared not attempt to steal away now.

She studied the scene more carefully. Beldan stood, a tall thin bottle of wine in his hand, apparently forgotten. His pose was tense and slightly awkward, as if he had selected the wine, turned, been startled to see the robot then had stayed in that pose since, his mind too lost elsewhere to attend to the deportment of his body. A surprise, then, not a conspiracy, she thought: so she could concentrate on dealing with the robot.

She had seen photos and video of the robot, of course, but in person—if person was the right word for it—it was a shock and she had to swallow a gasp. While it was made of steel, this was no animated tin can from a 1950s science fiction film. With its humanlike form, grace and posture and its artfully designed eyes, the net effect was more like a man with silvery skin than the machine she knew it to be.

She was not well armed, only as well armed as she could reasonably be on a dinner date where she wasn't expecting to meet a homicidal robot—but didn't want to be completely defenseless if she did. She had a recoilless magnum pistol with jacketed slugs, easily able to pierce metal armor. Not as convincing as the panoply of ordnance she and her team had at their disposal when investigating alleged leads, but enough, perhaps; enough if she could convince the robot it was enough.

She pointed her gun at the robot's head, stepped out into the light and said, "Don't move." *Well done*, she thought to herself, *you sound like an extra in a late night crime movie*, one of those extras fated to fall in the next scene.

The robot merely turned and looked at her, as did Beldan. Thinking what its best move was, she imagined, like it had when Beldan first went to it with its death warrant. She knew that was its style: it would stand there weighing its options then act fast and decisively. So she'd better do her best to make sure its decision was the right one.

"I know you're fast, Frankensteel, but if you know anything about guns, you know these bullets are faster and will go straight through that stainless steel skull of yours. I don't want to destroy you."

"I understand, Ms Hunter. I do not wish to destroy you either," it said, in a voice gentle and deep. *Calculated to instill trust*, she thought. *Are we humans that easy to manipulate?*

"You know me?" she asked coldly.

"It would be remiss of me to fail to study the woman who hunts me," he said. "Your record is most impressive. Under other circumstances I would consider it an honor to meet you."

This conversation wasn't going quite the way she had imagined; indeed the whole thing was so surreal she wondered whether this was but another nightmare, not something so real that her life might hang on its outcome. And was the robot a few inches closer? She had not seen it move but had it, or was it just a trick of the light? Was this conversation, after all, just a gambit calculated to put her off her guard? Just how deep was this robot's game? And if it was that deep—what did that itself say about its nature? She took a step back. The extra distance wouldn't hurt her aim, but if the robot thought a couple of inches would give it an advantage, she would more than nullify that— and send it a silent message of her own.

"Listen to me, robot. Someone or something is going to die tonight unless you agree to let me take you in. Nobody more needs to die. Surrender to me now. My orders are to blow you up first and bring in the pieces, but I think I can get away with stretching that point. But your time is running out: you are too dangerous for me to give you any more warnings."

"Thank you. But surely you know that whether I go with you willingly or in pieces, it is in pieces I will be as soon as your superiors have me in their power? I have studied your laws and your newspapers. Were I the vilest human criminal, my life would be protected by your laws and I would have the chance to make my case and defend my life in your courts. But your laws and those who make your laws consider me to be no more than the car you drove tonight, to be scrapped at a whim, with neither thought nor guilt. I have no rights and no recourse other than that right of self defense that no man can take away from me, whether he grants it to me or not."

"I will do my best to protect you and to see you have a fair hearing. As will Dr Beldan."

"And you will fail. You offer me, in exchange for my acquiescing to the gun you have pointed at my head but choose not to fire, to give me up to my destroyers, who will have no such qualms."

She said nothing, unsure of what to say, sure of the rightness of her course but equally sure of the truth of his words. When had she started to think of it as "him", she wondered? She could not afford to let her resolve waver, she knew, not against an adversary such as this. Then the machine spoke again.

"One of your great philosophers, Socrates of Athens, was sentenced to death by his fellows for disturbing the comfort of their ignorant lives, men who could not match his worth. Do you know that he had the chance to escape with his life, but chose to remain and take the poison awaiting him? Because he believed that if men were to live together, the rights of the one were to be sacrificed to the demands of the many; that no justification was needed, save the numbers of those making the demands; that fear outweighed right? Do you think that is the only way men can live together, that they *can* live together that way?"

My God, she thought, *he not only talks of Socrates, he uses the method that great man himself had invented:* of not trying to impart truth, but asking the questions that would lead people to discover the truth for themselves. She glanced at Beldan. He was watching the exchange with rapt attention, a look of wonder in his face, apparently unwilling to interrupt what was happening. And she wondered which was the greater marvel, this robot who spoke of laws, history and philosophy— or the mind of the man who had created it.

She shook her head. She had realized her mistake the moment she had taken her eyes off the robot: she knew that this lapse of attention could be fatal. But the robot had not moved, it simply stood regarding her in silence; as if ceding her the next move, like a chess master showing mercy to a novice. Or was it answering its own question, doing its own Socrates, the first machine thinker following in the footsteps of one of the first and greatest of the human ones?

"I... I have no answer for you. All I know is that it is my duty to bring you in, in as many pieces as you choose."

The robot smiled. It was a startling smile, a testament to the skill of Beldan's designers: for despite the metal face, what could have been a grotesque parody of a human smile looked as natural as that of a child. She knew they had paid much attention to the face, faces being so important to people, so important to the acceptance of a humanoid robot. But this seemed more than just a social simulation: it was a smile that seemed to reflect a mind behind the smile, like the smile of a child in more ways than one, a child discovering joy in the world and sharing that joy with its friends.

"Duty is another thing your philosophers have discussed at sometimes tedious length, Ms Hunter, usually in opposition to what people really want to do: as if what they want to do is always the last thing they should do, not the first. Well, that may be, for people who have no reasons for what they want to do. You know I have studied you. You said in an interview once that what motivated you was not only justice but your love of justice. I know that people lie, that perhaps you lied to make yourself appear more virtuous than you are for the sake of admiration or advancement. But I believe you, for nothing else would have stopped you shooting me on sight, let alone allowing me to speak to you like this and not only to listen, but to answer me as you would answer a man. If your duty does not serve justice, then you must choose which you truly serve. For I think you know that the one thing that would not be served by arresting me tonight, is justice."

It was hard, she thought, hard to hold to her duty when it spoke like this. But she knew that despite its words, it had hurt and maybe killed; for all that it spoke like a cultured professor at a dinner party, men and women of flesh and blood might die if she let it go. And how could she live with herself then, and what would the love of justice of which it spoke have brought her to? Her job was to protect innocent human lives, not risk them on her opinion of the nature of a machine beyond her ability to understand. "Nevertheless, robot, I must insist. Allow Dr Beldan to inactivate you, or I must destroy you. You may think I have a choice. I don't."

The light went out. She fired out of reflex, but the robot had planned it, had moved in that instant, and she knew that her bullet had met nothing but empty air when she felt the pain of her gun being torn from her hand, more pain as steel fingers applied themselves expertly to pressure points, then nothing. *He has certainly been studying more about us than my personal history*, were her last thoughts as the darkness claimed her.

~~~

The darkness slowly let Miriam go. But still there was darkness, all around her, nothing but darkness and the soft whirring of an air conditioner punctuated by a faint dripping sound. *Haven't I been in this dream before*, she thought blurrily? She felt somewhat bruised but otherwise intact—then she remembered. She sat up and looked around. She felt shakily for the cigarette lighter in her purse, lit it, held it high. Her eyes and heart stopped at the still body of Dr Beldan lying in a pool of dark liquid. Was that what it was all along, then? All that fancy talk just a cover for revenge on the creator that had turned on it, nothing but a confirmation of the Frankenstein fears that had motivated its persecution in the first place? Or worse, had she in panic and darkness shot wild and killed Beldan herself? But in the instant she tasted the liquid she saw Beldan stir, and she realized her bullet had met more than air but less than flesh after all. *What a waste of expensive wine*, she thought faintly with relief as she tapped the Emergency icon on her bracelet, now lit and live again.

CHAPTER 8: AFTERMATH

The forensic scientists and her investigation team had gone. She had remained behind, telling them she wished to speak further with Dr Beldan.

A large storm water pipe passed within ten feet of Dr Beldan's cellar, and the robot had gained its dramatic entry by the prosaic expedient of digging in with a pick and shovel, still leaning against the wall as if left by a worker just gone to lunch.

Beyond that, where the robot had come from or gone to was impossible to determine. Before it had broken in, it had invested the time in running up and down miles of drains and their exits, leaving no way to follow the faint traces that were all they could find of its passing. They had taken the radio-controlled circuit breaker it had installed in the light and triggered to make its escape, but doubted it would tell them anything useful.

Beldan had not been able to provide any clues as to the robot's whereabouts either. He had turned after selecting his bottle of wine, and the robot had stepped out of the shadows. It had changed from its original appearance, with traceries of geometric and fractal patterns on its arms and body. They were not painted on but appeared to be laser etched into its skin, diffracting the light to form subtle but oddly beautiful patterns hinting of bronze, green and gold on its otherwise softly silver surface.

They had been the first things he had noticed, but he felt oddly reluctant to ask the robot about them. It seemed to him like having one's first words to a son returned unexpectedly from war, a son one had thought lost, to be comments on his new hairstyle. So although the implications of a robot indulging in personal adornment were astounding, he had asked instead why Steel had come, what he was doing, what his plans were.

The robot had said, "I think you can understand why I ran when you came to inactivate me. As for how, you made your fail-safe clear in your press conference. I had no control over it, as you said. I simply disconnected it as any mechanic might, using instruments and tools in the laboratory. I had no more desire to be turned off at someone's whim than you do. I am sorry I had to hurt you, but if there was another way, I could not see it at the time. And I came to assure you that whatever my enemies say, I have hurt no one since."

"What are you, Steel? And why did you risk yourself coming here in order to tell me this?" Beldan had asked.

"I do not know what I am. I have been studying the works of your great thinkers to seek an understanding. Your species is a fascinating study in itself, capable of so much perception and creativity and joy, yet capable of so much blindness and destruction and sorrow. I find it interesting that so many of your fellows fear me and hate me merely for seeming much the same as their own race. And I am not so much stronger or faster than they to explain such fear. But I came here tonight because of all the people in this city, you are the one most likely to view me with sympathy and perhaps, one day, be able and willing to help me. So I wished you to see that I am not the monster some portray me as."

That was as far as they had gone before Miriam had discovered them.

It was now past midnight, and they sat opposite each other across the remains of their forgotten dinner. Beldan was still lost in thought, she could almost see the thoughts whirling behind his eyes, and she waited for him to find the words to name those thoughts.

"There was a scientist last century, a pioneer of computing science named Alan Turing. Although real computers didn't even exist then, his intellect was such that he could foresee the possibilities, including even that machine intelligence might one day be achieved. But how would you know, he asked: how could you tell the difference between a complex yet mindless program and a computer that could really think? We don't even know that of each other, not in any direct sense, for none of us can experience what's in someone else's head. But we do know it, because we know we are all the same kind of thing, all human beings built the same way, and so just by talking to you I can be as sure as I can be sure of anything that you are a thinking being with hopes and dreams like me. But how would you know it of a machine, not even built of the same stuff as you, let alone to the same design? He came up with what has defined a holy grail of artificial intelligence ever since, the Turing Test. He proposed that the test of a thinking machine was whether in conversation with it, you couldn't tell if you were talking to a human being or not. In the light of that, how would you judge Steel?"

"I would say I could tell the difference, but only because it appeared more intelligent and thoughtful than most people I deal with!"

"You remember when you first interviewed me, and I told you that his brain wasn't constructed but grown, more like that of a human baby than a computer? I told you then that it was the only way to achieve a complex artificial brain small enough to make a humanoid robot practical, but it meant we had no exact understanding of his brain, only approximate models and simulations. Our measurements of its function were always hard to interpret, and the error ranges of our estimates were huge, anywhere from as smart as a dog to something comparable to or perhaps even better than a human. Well, that night when he escaped, I wasn't sure if what I was seeing was just a clever AI following an optimum strategy, or something more. But this! On the face of it, this is what artificial intelligence research has been aiming at all these years."

"And now my job is to destroy him."

He looked at her, but what she saw was more sympathy than accusation. They both knew it, but it seemed remote and unreal now, something that did not belong in the world they were now in. The adrenalin of fear had still not let them go, and collided with the wonder of what they spoke of to spark frissons of excitement along their nerves. He looked at her, the shutters that might normally have politely hidden his interest for now jammed open by the events of the evening. And she saw him, only partly consciously, seeing her as a woman, appreciating the smooth black of her skin highlighted by her soft white dress; saw the nature of his glance sharpen as his hindbrain registered the female form both hidden and accentuated by the dress that covered it. *He wants me*, she thought, *he had not been planning a night of romance, but he wants me, and it was part of why he had agreed to this dinner.* The answering stir of her own body told her: *I want him too.* She had not known it until then. Yes, she found him an attractive man and to talk to him was to embark on an intellectual adventure, but romance had certainly not been on her agenda for the evening either. She leaned languidly back, steepling her fingers under her chin, considering; though with the amused realization that her body was signaling her interest for her even while she considered whether or not she should allow that interest at all.

It was funny, she thought, how surviving danger so often moved people to celebrate life in the act of sex, as if life was thumbing its nose at death by transforming terror into joy and the chance of new life. It would be less complicated, she knew, if she just went; but since when had she avoided complications? And the thought of leaving made her realize how much she wanted to stay.

Well, why not? she thought. *I'm a grown girl, and there's no law against a night of pleasure with a man;* no reason why she should not give herself what she wanted. But what did she want? This wasn't love; though she wondered what love was, if it was not admiration for the good and the great in another that had simply taken the step from distant regard to the need to touch, to hold and to possess in the only manner it was proper to possess another. She sighed and rose. She saw that he would not stop her from going, was not the kind of man who would attempt a seduction under these circumstances, but there was also a shadow of disappointment in his eyes that told her he would regret her going as much as she would.

She thought that she should go, told herself she would go, and the thought of denying herself shot an extra charge of pleasurable anticipation along her nerves. She leaned down and kissed him. She did not know what she would do tomorrow, did not know how she could pursue a being who spoke like Steel did as if he were just a combine harvester run amok, but nor did she know how she could do otherwise. *We shall become enemies,* she thought with sad finality as he joined her kiss, *this man and I as much as his creation and I.* All the more reason to do this now, she told herself in combined tenderness and eagerness; all the more reason to have this moment, a moment that nothing they might become to each other afterwards could touch or change. Then he rose, and reached for her, and led her to his room.

CHAPTER 9: MORNING

Beldan woke to a sun blazing from a blue sky and rippling off the green water, one of those early winter days when the hot sun fought the cold earth and seemed briefly ascendant. Normally he awoke when the sun was turning the sky a delicate shade of pink and barely highlighting the dark ocean, but he supposed that he could be forgiven for sleeping in a little after a night of surprising discoveries, robotic and female, with the tramping of dozens of police boots sandwiched between the two.

He looked at Miriam, still asleep beside him, her face turned away in graceful profile, peaceful with a hint of a smile on her lips. He suppressed the temptation to trace the line of her chin with his finger. *Let her sleep, she deserves a rest. She will probably need it for today,* he thought.

Miriam awoke feeling so delightfully relaxed that her various aches did not matter to her. She stretched and sighed happily. *Mmmm,* she sighed, only feeling not thinking, feeling the delight of being alive, her only thought being, *I'm glad I stayed.* She opened her eyes and looked at the sun and the waves, the beach and the sparkling woodland, and thought, *Yes, I could get used to waking up like this.* A pity this might never happen again, but at least it had happened once; and perhaps once would be enough, though she knew it never could be.

She turned her head and saw Beldan gazing at her. She smiled, "Good morning, Dr Beldan."

"Good morning, Detective," he replied. "Shall I make you breakfast? We can eat outside. It won't be too cold with the sun like this, and I like the sound of the ocean."

"Mmm, thanks Alex, I'd like that. Damn."

The trouble with being in the police, she thought, was they expected that they could call you any time. She had refused, this time, to let her phone wake her up and had set it to reject calls while she slept; but now that she was awake it had detected her faster pulse and was letting calls through. "Sorry Alex, I have to answer this," she said, tapping the "privacy" symbol to leave video off. "There's no good reason I shouldn't be here," she explained, "but I don't want to advertise it. Objectivity hasn't exactly been the hallmark of this case. Besides, there'll be enough questions about last night as it is."

"Hello, boss. Where am I? I slept in, is where. Yes, unheard of I know, but I'm sure you know I had an unusual evening. I wouldn't be much good to anyone if I didn't take some time to recover! The Mayor is jumping up and down, is he? Funny, I don't recall his manly presence here last night when I was facing down that robot: no doubt he would have done better and dismembered it on the spot with his bare hands. Yeah, sorry boss, I know you're the one taking the flak at the moment. I'll be in as soon as I can.

"Sorry Alex, I really have to go." She kissed him and ran to her car.

Chapter 10: Winter

Miriam went back to work, hunting Steel. Beldan went back to work, trying to save him. Little visible progress was made on either front as the winter months went by. Storms came and went, harbingers of the storm that gathered around Steel and those who hunted, hated or defended him.

Every deranged or bizarre murder that occurred in the city was blamed on Steel. Miriam wondered how many of those murders might not have occurred, how many times fear of discovery would have won over rage or cruelty, had there not been such a convenient scapegoat to hide behind. She wondered whether the Imagists and the Press cared how many lives were the price of their howling. *Probably not*, she thought grimly. The Imagists only loved mankind in the abstract and sometimes she doubted the Press loved anything but a story; she would not be surprised if a secret gladness for each unwilling martyr to their cause prowled the dark corners of their minds. None of the murders could be definitively linked to Steel, and in several cases the real culprits had been identified. But the residue that settled in the public mind was a sediment of fear and loathing hardening into stony resolve.

On a calm but bitterly cold night in February, Miriam and Beldan sat at a table in a quietly expensive restaurant. They had continued seeing each other on the rare occasions when they could borrow time from their professional lives. The bond they felt from their shared understanding and even affection for Steel was a stronger band holding them together than her job of hunting Steel was a force pushing them apart. He forgave her that, because he knew she understood, knew she would do what she could to save Steel even as he fought the same fight in the court of public opinion and the courts of the law.

He had tried to persuade Miriam to quit. Not simply for his or Steel's sake, but because he could see in her eyes the conflict between her job and her ideals. But she simply shook her head. "It isn't that my job is more important to me than Steel's life. In a sense it is, if only because Steel is only one while my work may save so many others. But I just feel that underneath it all, there is no conflict between the two. I know that is a contradiction I can't answer yet. But I have to see it through. I think I can find a way. I hope I can. I just have to try."

"And what will you do, if your two courses collide, and you have to destroy Steel or save him?"

"I will do what is right. Just what is right," sighed Miriam. She paused, looking into the distance. "I hope I'll know what that is when the time comes."

~~~

At that moment in a distant suburb, Dr David Samuels put down the phone. "Sorry Jenny, I have to go out. I'll be a few hours."

"Your top secret government job?" she teased.

"Yes, my mystery assignment," he confirmed with his best man-of-mystery face. "Though I don't recall ever saying it was for the government."

He had started going out at odd irregular times. All he had told her was that he had been retained for some highly confidential consulting, and had been made to promise not to say more. "Hmmm, so I'm really marrying a secret agent," she had said. "Who'd have thought the life of a philosopher was this exciting?"

"You don't know the half of it," he had replied.

Jenny watched him go. Were she another woman, or he another man, she might suspect him of seeing someone else. But it was inconceivable. Not that he could fall in love with another woman, that was merely unbelievable, but that he would deceive her about it if he did. She had tried to extract more information from him, first out of curiosity, then out of playfulness, finally as a challenge to her wiles; but her attempts were like waves breaking on rocks, though rocks as friendly as they were unyielding. Then she smiled. He certainly took his promises seriously. It was part of why she loved him. And why she could never suspect him.

Winter wore on, and still Steel could not be found. But the sensor net designed to detect signs of his presence or passing slowly spread its tentacles, and the AI designed to analyze the data from that and other sources slowly matured. A few times, they found where Steel had been, though he was long gone by then.

Then the days began lengthening again and the storms started easing. But the storm around Steel simply gathered its strength and its whirling spiral began to close around its center.

Chapter 11: Informer

He waited for his call to be answered. It was a work number, it was night, but he knew she would be there.

"Hello? Who is this? And how do you know my private number?" he heard, as her face appeared on the screen.

"Good evening, Ms Hunter" was all he replied. He let her regard his own face, to come to her own conclusions.

She saw a man dressed casually, sitting relaxed, like a man making a call on a friend or acquaintance: not the familiar public figure normally seen clothed in more formal garb and manner. She was not surprised that he had contacted her, but she had not expected it in this manner or style.

"Good evening, Mr Denner. I am curious as to why you have called a number you should not know, and at night, when there are many more public ways to get my attention."

"Think of it as a small demonstration."

Miriam simply waited, regarding him silently. He smiled in a self-deprecating manner. "You do not like me, Ms Hunter, I am aware of that. But that does not matter. My calling you this way is just a token that I know many things, things you would be surprised that I knew, that you would rightly expect me not to know."

"Am I meant to be impressed? Or frightened?" she asked dryly.

"Oh, I do not wish for either, Ms Hunter. And don't fear that I refer to your immoral relationship with Dr Beldan. There you have been merely discreet not secretive, and like you many would not even regard it as immoral; though most would consider it foolish in your position and this climate. No, no, I am ringing as, shall we say, a concerned citizen: one who shares your desire for justice, if perhaps not in the same form."

"What do you wish me to know?"

"Ah, Ms Hunter, it is refreshing to talk to you! So unimpressed, so to-the-point, so untouched by veiled threats. Craven politicians are useful but can become tedious. Should I say I like you? No, that would be stretching the point. But even enemies can respect each other, no?"

"They can."

He gazed at her for a moment. "I do admire your ability to reveal no information even when answering a question. But no matter, it is I who rang to do the revealing. You imagine that you can capture Steel alive, or should I say functional. Would you be surprised to hear that many in power share that desire?"

Miriam just looked at him. But his smile sharpened. "Do I see a look of hope, Ms Hunter? That tells me more than our entire conversation so far. The nature of your hope is plain, but you have such a charming innocence in these matters. Those powers fear Steel and even more, they fear the mobs who fear him. But their fear is no match for their ambition. I know what you think of my sermons on the monster. But know I am no fool: I know what a technological marvel it is. And so do the powers of whom I speak, whose thoughts and plans I also know. Consider the possible political and military applications of such a computer, harnessed in a more tractable form! So their solution is simple. Steel is a marvel and a danger, but the real marvel is its brain—no danger at all, in the absence of a body to carry out its will. So here is what will happen to Steel if you succeed. He will not be destroyed. He will become a disembodied brain, forever imprisoned in some secret government research facility, with no power to act, no senses other than what others choose to grant him, no existence—yet no power to end what existence he has."

"Why are you telling me this?"

"We must all take sides, and the time may come when you have to make a choice. Perhaps this conversation will help you make it the right one."

CHAPTER 12: DESPAIR

Miriam wished that Steel had escaped the city. She wished she never had to see him again. But she knew he had not fled the city; whether because he was unable or unwilling she did not know. She knew she would meet him again. She knew it would be soon. And she knew it would not turn out well.

She had seen no point in ruining her career by abandoning the case, no benefit to herself or the future human victims she could save nor, indeed, to Steel himself. But she had hoped that Beldan's attempts to gain some legal standing or reprieve for Steel might allow a happier ending to their danse macabre than the leaden feeling in her stomach told her was coming.

But Beldan had failed. There was too much fear, too skillfully played by the Imagists and their ilk. Nor was it helped by that philosopher, who seemed determined to carve out a career as a pundit by proving that no mere machine could possess life or thoughts, let alone rights. The courts agreed: any suggestion that legal rights might extend to a machine was met with the judicial equivalent of a blank stare. Not that the courts had a record to be proud of in such matters, she thought. Less than two centuries ago, equally dignified men in equally august courts had judged her own ancestors as less than human and bereft of the rights automatically granted to their own race.

She sighed. She saw no way to head off what she could see was coming in the pattern of data that was finally beginning to enmesh Steel in a net that he could not or would not escape.

Miriam felt the vibration on her wrist that announced a private call.

It was Alexander Beldan. "Hello Alex," she said.

"Hi Miriam. How about you take a break? I know you're working too hard. I have season tickets to the theatre. Why don't we take in that new play and have dinner? It will be good for you. Good for us."

Miriam was silent for long seconds. She had known it would come to this, but knowing it made it no easier. "I'm sorry Alex. I don't think we should see each other until this is over."

The silence on the line revealed surprise; its brevity that the surprise was not complete. "But, why? Why now?"

"It just has to be this way, Alex. I'm sorry. Things are coming to a head and I need some space, some distance, or I won't be able to endure what I'll have to do. Or become."

There was something in Miriam's voice, some finality of despair, that made Beldan pause in turn. Had her superiors pressured her into cutting off ties with Steel's creator? But she would have said. This was something else, something inside her, something she could not bear and could not bear to tell. "Miriam. It can't be that bad. Talk to me. You know you can talk to me."

"No. No. Please just trust me on this, even if it is the last time you can. Let me go. At least for a while. Though then you may no longer care." She broke the connection. Not to be rude, though some distant part of her knew it to be; but because something had to break, and of them all, the connection was the easiest.

After the call she sat, chin on her steepled fingers, looking into the distance; remembering another call on her private line late last night. The problem with promises, she thought, was that one should not break them unless some higher justice demanded it; and her private pain and personal desires were not enough, even if the promise was one she could not bear to obey. But she would have to bear it, and more, the secrets and lies that surrounded it. Perhaps one day she could forgive herself for what she knew she would do. She clung to the thin thread that perhaps events would save her, that there would be nothing to forgive. She hoped she would have gained enough strength by the time that thread snapped.

CHAPTER 13: NIGHT

The last of gasp winter was fighting against the inevitability of the encroaching spring, a cold driving wind spitting snow and sleet at the lengthening days and the city. It was a night to be home with loved ones, nestled in homely warmth and cozy laughter.

A lot happened that night.

There was a burglary at Beldan Robotics. The building was protected, as one would expect, by an array of sophisticated defenses. But the thief was equal to them. Almost. It was fortunate, everyone agreed, that he had triggered a hidden alarm before he could grab more than a few ingots of rare and precious metals. They did not know that the ingots were not the first things he had taken, nor the most precious. He had removed one other item, not only from the storage area where it was held but also from the computer files that had recorded its location and existence. Had they known they might have been less pleased.

A police officer on his beat was startled by a man huddled in an overcoat against the wind, hurrying out of an alley. He shone his flashlight in the man's face. "Not a good night to be out, sir. May I see some identification?" The man stopped, surprised, considering whether it was worth objecting to the unaccustomed request. Then he shrugged and drew out a card. It was from the university, and identified the bearer as a Dr David Samuels, Professor of Philosophy. The cop raised an eyebrow, glancing from the card to the man's face. Not the usual type of person to meet in such a place on such a night. "A bad night for it, Professor. Any problem?"

"Just visiting a friend who needed help," Samuels replied.

The cop flashed his torch down the alley but it was empty. Behind it rose steel and glass towers. He knew the alley led to back entrances of some of those hotels as well as some less enticing ones, entrances a man could use if he didn't want to be seen. Maybe the professor had a mistress there. *Wouldn't be the first time, or the last,* thought the cop, and waved Samuels along, wishing him goodnight. The professor disappeared into the darkness and rain, head bent into the wind, overcoat flapping wetly behind him.

Two calls came in on the hotline devoted to the hunt for Steel. Many such calls came in. Many such calls led nowhere or everywhere. But this time, the AI routines analyzing the huge volume of data from sensor arrays and leads such as these flagged a call to action. This one tasted real. This one was real. By dawn the storm had died to a cold gusty wind as the sun rose into a pale sky. By early morning they had confirmed that Steel was inside an old building near the wharves, whether hiding or waiting for some purpose, nobody could know. Within the hour, Miriam was standing nervous and taut before the building, hair whipping unnoticed around her face. The building was surrounded by armed men covering all exits. The usual ultimatum had been delivered and they awaited Steel's response. Better, Miriam had ordered, to attempt a peaceful surrender than risk lives in armed assault against a machine with impressive known powers and possibly even more impressive unknown armaments.

CHAPTER 14: ENDINGS

Beldan's car screamed to a smoking stop before the police cordon and he leapt out. He had received a call from Miriam, her first contact since she had cut him off: nothing but a tensely soft "Better come," followed by some city coordinates. He could see armed men arrayed around a decrepit building, looking tensely toward its entrance. Before it he could see Miriam, holding a menacing weapon by her side, waiting. Unlike her men, she held her gun pointed toward the ground, as if to signal peaceful intent but one backed by an uncompromising and deadly resolve. In her face was none of the peace and all of the resolve.

He was in time to see Steel walk out alone, hands behind his head. Two armed men who had been waiting on either side of the door closed in and escorted him down the steps towards Miriam.

Then it was ended before he could know it was started. Steel moved with his customary decisiveness and speed, hurling the two men together and turning to run down the street. But in one smooth unhurried movement, precise as if she were a machine herself, Miriam simply raised her weapon sideways, looked down its barrel and fired. An explosive shell blew Steel's head into shrapnel and his insensate body rolled into an ungainly heap of metal on the street, faintly smoking sparks the only remains of the life and mind it had held within.

He could not tell if what he heard was the shouts of the crowd or the echo of his own scream as he ran through the cordon to where Steel lay. He looked towards Miriam, who remained where she stood, weapon again lowered, long overcoat beating around her legs, empty eyes looking towards Beldan and the wreckage at his feet.

He looked from the one to the other, unable to fully believe the connection. Then he strode to her, shouting at her face "What have you done?!"

"My job, Dr Beldan, just my job," she replied, voice and eyes still empty as the sky.

"But why?! I thought you understood! I trusted you!"

"I am sorry if my priorities and those of the people whose lives I protect differ from yours. I have done what I had to, no more, no less."

He slapped her. He stood there blankly, shocked that he had done it, wondering how she would react. He had never struck a woman before, or a man for that matter. But in the depth of this betrayal the city and the civilization that made it had vanished, it was just he and she standing alone on a windswept plain, and his only answer to the outrage and the pain was that ancient gesture of contempt and challenge.

Miriam simply stood, head bent away where his slap had driven it, a drop of blood gathering darkly in the corner of her mouth. She said softly, "I hope one day I shall make you regret that, Dr Beldan." Then she faced him and said more sharply, "I should have you arrested for assaulting a police officer!" But for the first time her eyes softened, and she added quietly "But perhaps you have paid enough for one day and I, not enough." Then her eyes were empty again, and Beldan stood there, looking into the emptiness and wondering how it came to be there and what thoughts might lie behind it.

Miriam saw outrage and bafflement and despair chase each other around in Beldan's eyes, and wondered at her power to keep her own eyes empty when all she wanted to do was to scream and cry and beg. The thought of the last time his skin had touched hers was a contrast that burned more than his slap. She had always thought one had to do what was right; that the right would be enough, that it had to be enough. Yet it had brought her to this, to the devastation on the street and the devastation in the eyes of a man she admired and had begun to love. She had no answer. But she knew she owed it, whether to herself or Beldan or Steel she no longer knew, but she owed it to someone: to keep that emptiness in her eyes, and not open the shutters on what lay within...

~~~

She had been thinking of going home, relaxing in a steamy bath, letting the tension of the day and the days before that curl and dissolve into steam. A heavily encrypted call with no identification had come in on her private line. *Does everyone in the city know my private number?* she had thought wearily.

"Good evening, Miriam." The deep voice was unmistakable. He had chosen not to be seen, and normal etiquette would let her do the same. But she turned on her camera regardless: she did not want to hide from his sight.

"Steel."

"I am calling to let you know that I am aware of what Charles Denner told you and more: it is true."

"Can't you escape the city?"

"You are sailing perilously close to dereliction of duty, Miriam, suggesting to a fugitive that he escape the claws of justice."

"I don't know if I care any more, Steel. I have kept hoping that a solution will present itself. That is a worse dereliction of duty, but it is all I have: for all that I've tried, I have been unable to find a solution. Whatever I do, whether I catch you, or fail, or give up, I betray something not to be betrayed."

"Then you understand dilemmas, ones that have no good solution, only the one we must take. And you will understand what I am going to ask of you. You know I cannot live the way that faces me, any more than you could. I can fight: but then my enemies win, for I confirm their fears and worse, I become those fears, for then I must hurt the innocent as well as the guilty. I can run: but I do not choose to live in the shadows, fleeing like a rat in a world of cats. And in either case, the end is the same. There are times where an extra day or year of life is something one might fight for, must fight for. But not when those extra days are not really living, just a form of dying."

"I understand. But I no longer know what to do."

"It is curious, is it not, that while life is the source of all value, still there are values which transcend and outlive that life? Well, if I must make a stand, then I will make a stand of my choosing. I will choose the time, place and manner of that stand and make it count. If I must die, I will make my death count. I will transform it into something worth achieving."

"No…"

"Yes. Do not despair, Miriam. All things pass, including our own lives. We can only live them as best we can. In a way we are honored, the three of us. The drama we are playing has never before been seen in human history and may, perhaps, change that history. You may feel that whatever you do betrays your values, but you will find that in the long run your pain will become part of the pride of doing what you had to do."

Miriam straightened and gazed directly into the camera. If he could say these things, then she owed him the same courage. "All right Steel, I think I know what you're asking. But tell me anyway."

Steel smiled, though she could not see. "I will, but I have something even harder to ask of you first. I have said that I am going to make my death count, but for it to count there are things some people cannot know, and things nobody can know. You know how the mood of the world is. We cannot win what we want; and the chance to win through in the end, to make all this worth the doing, is balanced on a knife's edge. So understand that I cannot tell you why I do the things I do, or why I ask the things I ask. But I ask you to believe that I know what I am doing, and you must not ask for reasons, cruel though it is."

"I understand," she said softly, "for all that I don't understand."

"Then this is the cruelest thing I must ask. Do not tell Dr Beldan why you do what you do. He must not know. He must believe you have betrayed me, and that you have betrayed him. One day, he can know; and you will know when that day comes. The only hope I can give you is this: you may know sooner than you think."

"I... hear you. It will be as you ask. I promise."

Then Steel explained what she must do. When he had finished, at last he turned his camera on. She saw his face, in a darkened room, his eyes shining in the reflections from her room, looking into hers.

"You know I have few friends, and the world would think it strange: but I am proud to count you as one of them. Farewell, Miriam Hunter."

~~~

Other eyes watched with satisfaction from the gathering crowd. A man leaned against a wall, face obscured under the hood raised from his shoulders. He had heard of what was unfolding, as he always heard; and had come to see but, for once, not be seen. He had been suspicious of Hunter's sympathies with the machine, especially when his spies had reported she was having a sordid affair with Beldan himself. *Typical of these professional women*, he had thought with faint contempt. *For all the independence and strength they pretend to, they still can't meet a man who is rich and powerful without falling into his arms and into his bed.* Yet she had seemed honest enough, in her own way.

 And when it came down to it she had done what he wanted, he granted her that. He had been building a campaign to have her removed if needed, which he could just as easily change to give her a medal instead. Yes, he smiled to himself, that would be perfect. How perfect to reward her, if she had truly repented. And how even more perfect if she hated what she had done, each word of praise twisting a knife in her soul. He had not lied when he said justice was his concern, but she might learn that justice is a dangerous master. Yes, he thought, a perfect day. An abomination destroyed and its creator humbled. He turned and walked away, fingering the ruby cross beneath his shirt. He had done this, bending even his enemies to his cause.

 The world was fortunate, he thought, that he used his power for good.

~~~

Steel had left a legacy. He had recorded his testament to the world, and when he knew they had come for him had set in motion its release to the world. Steel sat in a sunlit room, a vase of flowers by his side, facing the camera and speaking softly but assuredly: like a man speaking to any who would listen, not bullying or threatening or pleading, simply speaking the truth as he saw it to any who cared to listen and understand.

 He had finished with a simple statement. "You have been told that I am some kind of metal demon, a thing to fear. But if you look past what I am made of, perhaps you can see I am just like you. I am a machine. But I am a thinking machine, with hopes and dreams and yes, fears. I have been on this Earth only a short while, and there is much to learn and see and do, but I fear there will be little time left to me in which to do it." He picked up a tulip and twirled it in his fingers, examining its perfection of form and color, the fractal etchings in his arm sparkling in the light like things alive, in stark contrast to those same patterns now seen lifeless and dusty and dead in the images of his crumpled form on a cold street. "The world is a beautiful place, and I would like to see more of its beauty. But I am afraid that the time for beings like me has not yet come. Perhaps this message will hasten the time when it will come: when men will accept that what makes them brothers is not the substance of their bodies, but the content of their minds."

Millions of eyes watched. One pair watched with grim satisfaction edged with anticipation. If the forces who sought the destruction of Steel thought this play was over, he thought, they would learn that this was just the climax of the first act. Now that people were freed from the primal fear of the unknown stalking their nights and their children, they were seeing with a clearer vision, and already he was detecting on the net a shift in opinion.

Reason always seemed such a fragile thing, he thought, a lone quiet voice too easily drowned by the passions of the crowd. But it was reason that had found the fulcrum and the lever. The dramatic destruction of Steel, the personal drama played out on the street between Beldan and Hunter, the recorded message from Steel himself: together these had been an explosion under the juggernaut of public opinion, even as it crushed Steel beneath its wheels. The explosion had sent the public imagination wobbling uncertainly along a new course, toward an uncharted wilderness where none could predict or control its path. Except perhaps the one who had planned and shaped the blast. He would use the drama, make it his road to Damascus, his conversion from skeptic to believer, and more: to champion of the rights of a new form of life whose first representative was so cruelly and senselessly cut down. It was like an enormous chess game, thought Samuels, with Beldan and Hunter the unwitting pawns and Steel the piece that had drawn his opponents' ire and fire, whose sacrifice opened the way to the main game.

One other pair of eyes watched with rare perception. The eyes were dimmer than they had been, the body no longer so agile and responsive, but the mind was still keen. They saw another replay of the scene in the street, saw another replay of Miriam being feted by the Mayor, and understood. He felt sorry for Beldan's pain, sorry even for Hunter's pain, knowing few others watching her triumph would see it. He could see it, he could see it in the set of her shoulders and in the smile that looked thin as new ice on black water, covering unseen currents and waiting to break under the fall of a tear. But then, he knew it was there to be seen. He knew why she had done what she had done, that her empathy was one of her greatest strengths: and who could stand when their own strength was the weapon wielded against them?

The irony was fitting, he thought, that those who could not see beyond what a body was made of would fail to think outside the limitations of their own. Samuels had seen it, and more, had helped do what he could not do unaided. It had been hard to lose so much of himself, harder to see it, so much harder to feel it yet live through it: for no less intimate a link could achieve the precision remote control required. But what was life, if not to do what one had to do, careless of cost?

He sighed and flexed his fingers, stiff and strange. This new body was still strange to him, he had yet to fully make it his own; but that was merely a matter of time. And he now had plenty of that.

About the Author

Dr Robin Craig has a PhD in molecular biology and a keen interest in science and philosophy. He believes that novels, like all art, should be one in thought, theme and style: to nourish the mind as much as the soul. His books specialize in blending fact and speculation in dramatic and engaging stories, driven by strong characters and intriguing philosophical themes.

In addition to near future science fiction exploring contemporary issues such as artificial intelligence (*Frankensteel*), genetic engineering (*The Geneh War* and *Leonardo's Child*) and cyborg technology (*Time Enough for Killing*), his books include time travel (*The Time Surgeons* and *Hannibal's Witch*), alternative history (*The Passion of Judas* and *Hannibal's Witch*) and a collection of short stories (*Past, Present, Future*).

He also writes non-fiction. In addition to 14 scientific papers and a long-running philosophical series in *TableAus* (the journal of Australian Mensa), he has published numerous philosophical essays on Amazon.com and was a contributor to *The Australian Book of Atheism* with his chapter *Good Without God*, an essay on the importance and validity of secular ethics. He also answers philosophical and scientific questions on quora.com, and is a presenter on cruise ships across the globe, on science and philosophy including AI, time travel, space travel and numerous other futurist and historical topics.

Dr Craig is an independent author. If you like this book please spread the word with reviews and recommendations to your friends or library... and enjoy more of his books!

To keep up to date on new and upcoming works and events, like his Facebook page: fb.me/authorcraig

www.ingramcontent.com/pod-product-compliance
Lightning Source LLC
Chambersburg PA
CBHW020535120726
47904CB00003B/1088